ANOTHER MODEST PROPOSAL

BY LAWRENCE ROWE

FICTION

The Founding Fathers Return

The Tesla Paradox

NONFICTION

Bubblenomics

Bubblenomics 2

VISIT LAWRENCE ONLINE

LawrenceRowe.com

ANOTHER MODEST PROPOSAL

Lawrence Rowe

New York

Printed in the United States of America by MDR Press.

ISBN-13: 978-0-9767668-8-9

Another Modest Proposal may be purchased at special bulk quantity discounts for educational or promotional use. For information, e-mail: specialmarkets@lawrencerowe.com.

First paperback printing: February 2017.

10 9 8 7 6 5 4 3 2 1

For the hungry.

"There are people in the world so hungry that God cannot appear to them except in the form of bread."

—Mahatma Gandhi

"Some people think luxury is the opposite of poverty. It is not. It is the opposite of vulgarity."

—Coco Chanel

"Once poverty is gone, we'll need to build museums to display its horrors to future generations. They'll wonder why poverty continued so long in human society—how a few people could live in luxury while billions dwelt in misery, deprivation and despair."

—Muhammad Yunus

"Experience declares that man is the only animal which devours his own kind; for I can apply no milder term to the governments of Europe, and to the general prey of the rich on the poor."

—Thomas Jefferson

Contents

ANOTHER MODEST PROPOSAL

Lawrence Rowe

2017

ANOTHER MODEST PROPOSAL

For Preventing the Residents of Least-Developed Countries from Being a Burden to Developed Nations, and for Making Them Beneficial to Humanity.

It is ghastly to visit impoverished nations and see hordes of refugees feigning subsistence. Citizens of least-developed countries languish listlessly, attracting flies like piles of horse dung, their rib cages so discernable that x-rays seem to be at work. Sapped of vitality by malnutrition, these emaciates cannot be employed gainfully and live in a perpetual state of neglect.

This haunting poverty is a global epidemic. Each year, millions on Earth die from malnutrition. Mass starvations in least-developed countries have become almost commonplace. As anyone clubbing in Rome can attest, the Earth's population is growing at an alarming rate, and most of this overproduction is occurring in least-developed countries, meaning the bulk of humanity will continue to subsist in a primitive state as its forbearers have. Whoever could derive a reasonable, fair, and inexpensive method to provide sustenance to these impoverished individuals would be doing them, and humanity as a whole, an enormous service.

3

I have therefore focused my energies on this problem for a significant span of time, giving the matter thorough consideration. I have examined all attempted solutions and a multitude of theoretical possibilities. All remedies attempted to date have been grossly ineffective. All solutions that have been proposed make unrealistic assumptions and are destined to fail. We must be blunt about these failures, confront them candidly, and move on to the implementation of effective remedies such as my proposal. It is the most sensible, and certainly the most humane, solution to this distressing and delicate problem.

Before outlining my proposal and its merits, a discussion of previous efforts and why they have failed is necessary. A framework for new proposals that precludes repetition of past mistakes must be established.

Unlike residents of least-developed countries, who are thoroughly desensitized to suffering and poverty due to repeated exposure, residents of developed nations are consistently and unequivocally appalled by it. Not content to merely buffer themselves behind their insulated walls of wealth, they candidly face the problem, developing a thorough understanding of the plight of refugees in impoverished countries.

This unwillingness to let poverty become a distant abstraction leads to a laudable attitude; residents of developed nations are wholly sympathetic to the cause of eradicating world hunger, as evidenced by their significant individual sacrifices towards this end. In an admirable display of altruism, they forsake necessary material possessions and live even more modestly so that others do not starve.

Unfortunately, some misguided individuals still suggest that increased financial involvement by developed nations of the world is the solution to global poverty. This panhandling is inconsiderate to those nations that already donate so much to this worthy cause. Insinuations that developed nations are not presently expending maximum efforts to end global poverty are insulting. The reason developed nations do not give more to help the less fortunate has nothing to do with a lack of compassion. The problem is not selfishness, greed, or indifference, but scarcity. Developed nations have no more resources to spare. They have been bled dry through endless donations that never seem to help the problem. It is certainly not an exaggeration to say that residents of developed nations have given all they can, their tremendous sacrifices are not enough, and no other answer presents itself.

We must squarely confront the fact that the collective, worldwide effort to banish poverty has failed. The prosperous peoples of the Earth bonded together with the same sense of urgency mustered to defeat the Axis in World War II, embarking on a kind of Manhattan Project for poverty. Humanity unfortunately failed to achieve the critical mass needed for total victory. In hindsight, with the wisdom that comes only from experience and effort, it is abundantly clear that the problem of global poverty is too gargantuan for simple charity or redistribution of resources to be viable solutions.

Once the problem is recognized as something more complex than resource misallocation and the depravity and greed of developed nations and their residents, and we abandon the pretense that the efforts of developed nations can have any effect on global poverty, new paradigms based on viable and realistic solutions can be examined. In acknowledging that developed nations have practically impoverished themselves in their crusade against global poverty and are incapable of rendering additional assistance, we infer that realistic solutions must not depend on outside assistance. Paradoxically, this realization gives cause for optimism. For we then understand that least-developed countries can no longer sit by idly waiting for handouts from the rest of the world. The old proverb about giving a man a fish or teaching him to fish is especially relevant here. Feeding starving people in least-developed countries would simply create a destructive dependency. In fact, from a certain viewpoint, the lack of developed-nation assistance can be considered an unusual brand of compassion. It will force least-developed countries to adopt rugged—highly rugged—individualism. They will finally realize they must help themselves in the battle against their endemic poverty.

My intention is far greater than the simple alleviation of poverty, however. I intend to help residents of least-developed countries not just survive, not just obtain enough resources to subsist, but develop their countries, over the long run, into a state of advancement comparable to other civilized nations. Only then can they live life with the vigor, efficiency, generosity, and compassion that are the trademarks of developed nations.

I shall now outline my proposal, which I hope the reasonable and compassionate citizens of Earth will accept in its entirety without objection: Each family in least-developed countries will become a self-sufficient herd. Whenever hunger strikes, a family member will simply be sacrificed, prepared to taste, and ingested.

In both caloric value, and overall flavor and enjoyability, human flesh and organs are wholly superior to the bugs and scavenged rodents that make up the bulk of the present diet in least-developed countries. Cannibalism is the most efficient solution to the problem because homo sapiens are the only readily available resource in impoverished regions. Since least-developed countries produce almost nothing but people, what other resource can they use as a starting point if they are to rely only on themselves? This argument should have a particularly strong appeal to residents of developed nations who admire capitalism and the enormous wealth it creates. Capitalism is predicated upon efficient utilization of resources, which is a hallmark of my plan.

Let us proceed efficiently then with an examination of my proposal's numerous practical advantages, and its execution. First, it would make food supplies immediately available on a continuous basis. Second, since no external aid will be necessary to provide the nutrition, and it uses a plentiful, replenishable resource, the long-term sustainability will be assured. Third, population growth and excessive birth rates, considered a negative in the present system, disappear: more offspring are simply more food. Fourth, since each group of progeny is both a family and a herd, the need for infrastructure to transport food stores is eliminated.

The United States Recommended Daily Allowance (USRDA) is roughly 2,000 calories per day. Though the average impoverished resident of a least-developed country would probably consider a quarter this amount gorging, we shall nonetheless assume ideals. The number of calories of sustenance the average human can provide must now be determined. This is a figure that varies person to person depending on factors such as weight, height, build, and body fat level, though, as with caloric requirements, averages can certainly be assumed. There being no previous statistical summary of large scale butchering of humans for food, I have employed dressing percentages common to other herd animals such as cattle and deer. Butchers inform me that roughly 70% of an animal's weight is used for ingestible material, not including hot dogs, pickled feet, and other derivative products made from waste. Though residents of developed nations often weigh more than 200 pounds, the average resident of a least-developed country is slimmer and slighter of build, due most probably to genetic differences; a developed-nation arm is like a drumstick, while a least-developed-country arm is little more than a wing. Taking this litheness into account and generously assuming a mean body weight of 100 pounds for residents of least-developed countries, we conclude that an average long pig would yield approximately 70 pounds of meat.

The exact nutritional content of human flesh and organs is also unknown. Assuming a caloric content for comparable lean game like pheasant or deer leads to an estimate of roughly 800 calories of energy per pound of human flesh. The feasibility and ultimate sustainability of this proposal is now easier to visualize. Each carved person can feed roughly 28 people per day at the United States

Recommended Daily Allowance! With at least one billion people suffering from malnutrition that stunts growth and is often fatal, and at least four billion subsisting at best, we find encouragement. Almost four billion people yielding 70 pounds of meat apiece at 800 calories per pound is 224 trillion calories! This is an enormous store of latent energy that has the power, and literally is the power needed, to end malnutrition and the senseless suffering resulting from it.

If the aforementioned propensity of impoverished individuals to consume less than the U.S. Recommended Daily Allowance is factored in, the yield per carved person would increase. Initially, bodies may weigh less, and later, once fed, perhaps more. This would require processing more or less people, as the fluctuating yield requires.

Though processing many people immediately after my proposal is implemented may seem like a disadvantage because it represents a squandering of future food stock, this apparent waste is offset by the fact that each person processed represents one less mouth to feed. And even skeptics must concede that the herds available for processing are large.

It is expected that the blood of disposed individuals will be drunk for nourishment, as the Maasai do with cattle, which is a yield increase not accounted for in conventional dressing percentage and caloric metrics. Human blood contains about 300 calories per pint. The average human has eight pints of blood, or about 2,400 calories of blood. Those inclined to disparage the accuracy of the dressing-percentage calculations presented above should be aware of this blood-calorie allowance.

One cattle farmer I spoke with worried that once residents of least-developed countries are eating regularly, they will become a stouter, beefier, Angus-like stock, body weight will increase, and more and more humans will have to be butchered because each body would require more calories. However, each butchered human will also be providing more calories. The concern in this situation that a population may outgrow its food supply is nonsensical. It is impossible for a population to outgrow a food supply when the population itself is the food supply, unless it is reduced to one weak-willed individual.

One critic of my proposal argued that residents of least-developed countries will respond to an excess of food as residents of developed nations have, by stooping to gluttony. The initial assumption in this argument, residents of least-developed countries eating regularly and obtaining adequate nutrition, has never occurred for any sustained period of time, except perhaps in distant antiquity. Suppositions about how residents of least-developed countries will respond to adequate nutrition are therefore mere conjecture.

Assuring there is enough meat to eat is not the only issue to consider. There are serious ethical and social questions raised by this plan, and I would be negligent if I glazed over them to make it more palatable.

Some social structure to accompany cannibalism is necessary, otherwise fights will arise over who is the entrée for a given day or meal. Fighting to determine ingestion order in a society's cannibalistic food chain may seem like a reasonable approach, but it induces several unacceptable inefficiencies and cruelties. The immorality of violence is a key consideration; a society should strive to exist in a state of peace and comfort, and day to day fighting is detrimental to this end. The energy expended fighting would increase the nutritional requirements of survivors. Fighting also results in random selection of victims. Butchering a woman who may reproduce and provide future food supplies is illogical and detrimental to the long-term wellbeing of the society. Likewise, the consumption of a child or young adult before they have reached maturity reduces the food yield that could have been derived had they been allowed to grow to full size.

Eating older males first may seem like a new breed of chauvinism, or some attempt to turn men and women against each other like praying mantises, but it is mere practicality. The capabilities and usefulness of individuals to the society or tribal structure should be the primary consideration in exemption from consumption.

Natural selection exists in nature, and one might ask why it should not also exist in a cannibalistic culture that approximates the competition of nature more explicitly than most other human societies. The major objection is human morality, a morality that compels our species, by virtue of reasoning capabilities that separate us from animals, to prevent avoidable suffering.

A set of protocols dictating a logical pecking order for consumption is thus indispensable. A situation in which cannibalism was allowed to exist without such protocols could only be described as cruel, perhaps even barbaric. Cannibalism must be enacted in a civilized manner.

Even with proper organization and planning, there are likely to be growing pains when my proposal is first adopted. The first humans used for food may be quite reticent. Nonetheless, democratic principles will win out. It is simply a matter of the needs of the many outweighing the needs of the few.

After the first few years, cannibalism will not be the atrocity mankind now views it as, but rather a way of life. Over time, the taboos presently associated with cannibalism will disappear and it will become, like exploiting the poor, just another industry.

Homo sapiens cannot live on a diet of meat alone. Though some impoverished individuals may turn to high-protein, low-carbohydrate weight-loss programs at some future date once an excess of food has facilitated obesity, an Atkin's-style, meat-only diet is inappropriate for individuals who have maximized weight loss through a regimen of involuntary starvation. Clearly, the grain, vegetable, and dairy products that are part of a balanced diet will be necessary. This need is addressed by my proposal. Scraps are an inevitable waste product when butchering corpses, and if utilized efficiently they can be the foundation of agriculture.

Though a human corpse might be devoid of scraps if it were carved and boiled away to create soup stock and the marrow were sucked out of the bones, corpses will not be used this efficiently in most cases. There will be waste.

Corpses contain nutrients. Buried corpses gradually release nutrients into the surrounding soil, enriching it. Huge numbers of corpses buried in one small region would have the cumulative effect, over time, of fertilizing the land.

Once fertilized by human cadavers, scraps, and entrails, as well as ammonia-rich feces and urine, the land can be used to grow crops that will provide other needed nutrients not found in human flesh. The year-round addition of corpses will keep the land fertile, especially if some sort of crop rotation system is utilized. Families can be expected to take care of fertilized soil because it was literally sown by a loved one. This spiritualistic and nostalgic association will be quite powerful.

As an aside, cemeteries have long been recognized as a waste of valuable acreage, and my proposal prevents this waste, converting them into arable farmland.

In the initial stages of this proposal, fertilization will proceed quickly because processing of corpses will be especially inefficient. The robust quantity of scraps produced will accelerate the creation of arable land when it is needed most.

This process of fertilizing land will be gradual, but nonetheless achievable. As more human remains are added to farmland each year, the arable land will slowly increase in size and the initial, tenuous self-dependence will grow more sustainable.

Hunger has one underestimated physiological byproduct: a lack of energy. Nourished residents of least-developed countries will have the vitality to begin constructing the implements of civilized society. At this stage of economic development, the human body will become a source of much more than mere nourishment. Human skin could be dried and stretched over fibulas lashed with tendons to make shelter. Utensils, tools, and weapons could be made from bones. Bowls for eating and storage could be made from skulls. Human tallow could be rendered and used to make soap and candles. Like American Indians that derived all their necessities from buffalo, residents of least-developed countries will be able to create an almost endless array of utilitarian necessities from each other. They will also never have to chase a herd or worry about locating it, a reality that would have made Native Americans redskinned with envy. An exception might be those few selfish, recalcitrant individualists who refuse to sacrifice for the greater good. As with other social norms, deviance will be punished punitively, in this case capitally. We need not be squeamish about facing this fact, and those that are can simply ignore it as they have been ignoring poverty itself.

Congregating near regions of self-fertilized land, herds will eventually forsake their nomadic existence and form organized communities. Living together in villages, our cannibals will begin their evolution towards developed-nation status through trade.

Trade would begin within villages in local markets and spread between villages. For example, a tall family whose fibulas are useful for the erection of shelter supports might trade with a large-craniumed family whose skulls make superior serving bowls.

A crude export market featuring human wares would soon arise. Whole human skulls could be tooled to uniformity, buffed, polished, and sold on world markets. Bone fragments could be made into wind chimes, dice, charm bracelets, and other easily-crafted wares. Admittedly, such wares are no match for the sophisticated products made in developed nations, and they cannot be expected to sustain economies for the long term, but they are a start. The export of hand-made and made-from-hand products can be used to thin populations in least-developed countries to tolerable levels while creating wealth that allows modern industries and infrastructure to be created.

The first modern production facilities would be human slaughterhouses. At last, implementation of state-of-the-art technology, true mechanization, and massive economies of scale could be realized in developing nations! It is reasonable to assume that these slaughterhouses would achieve an efficiency comparable to that of other butcher industries in developed nations. Tens of thousands of people could be processed each day!

As in the nomadic scenario, every part of the human body could be used to create marketable products at minimal cost. Conventional butchery offerings such as steak, chops, veal, sapien dogs, beef sticks, jerky, and humanwurst would be produced. Exotic delicacies such as tongues, eyes, breasts, and penises could be sold for gourmet preparation. Instead of shark-fin soup, Orientals might come to favor clitoris soup. Human fingers might replace chicken wings, easing the shortages and price increases of that increasingly popular appetizer. Other possible products include bones and skeletons for doctors' offices and classrooms, flesh for skin grafts, organs for transplants, hormones for medical applications, and real-flesh costumes for parties and Halloween. American food franchises may also wish to get in on the gravy train. For example, McDonald's could sell a humanburger, the McSapien.

One anthropologist the author spoke to who is also a musician suggested a ritual of playing the exposed ribs of family members like a xylophone just before their liquidation. After consumption, the rib cages of each family member could then be buffed and polished, have keys attached, and be marketed as xylophones. This would mandate the consumption of boneless rather than bone-in steaks, but such a concession is trivial when weighed against the overall value added.

An engineer the author consulted is adamant that crematoriums could be economically retrofitted with low-heat apertures that allow ovens to be converted into jerky makers. Some of this jerky could be eaten by loved ones at a funeral, as a token of affection and remembrance, and the rest of the body meat, including the internal organs, would be preserved for transport to least-developed countries. Heart, kidney, and jerky made from other organs is novel, and may fetch immense sums on retail markets.

This small list is a mere beginning; the variety of marketable products that could be created is as limitless as human decency itself.

Human meat would be less expensive than competing products like beef, pork, and poultry, making it competitive and highly sought after. After all, most farm animals in developed nations receive food, shelter, and medical treatment that human livestock in least-developed countries do not. Not providing these superfluous luxuries to the human livestock in least-developed countries will facilitate a substantial cost savings and allow least-developed countries to offer a product comparable in quality to other meats at a much lower price.

Advertising campaigns could be launched to increase sales. The superior texture, flavor, and price of human flesh could be lauded. The humanitarian nature of the products will be explained, so that consumers in developed nations realize purchasing products made from human flesh literally saves lives. Compassionate residents of developed nations would undoubtedly be moved by such advertisements, increasing their consumption of human products dramatically to aid in the crusade against malnutrition.

Marketing campaigns that highlight the humane conditions for human production would also be useful. Since all human meat produced by least-developed countries would be considered free roaming or free range, the livestock is not fed hormones, and starving residents of least-developed countries have no access to processed foods containing pesticides or preservatives, it would be some of the mostly purely organic meat in the world. Organic, free-range human would be an attractive alternative to other meats as concern about ethical treatment of livestock and a healthy diet continues to increase.

Cooking shows, that fascinating fixation of the well-fed and obese, could be used to normalize cannibalism. Gordon Ramsay could host a competitive cooking show entitled Cannibal Cookoff, and his no-nonsense attitude would be especially helpful in inducing hesitant neophytes to butcher a person for the first time. Ideally, the loser in each round would be the entrée in the next round, which jibes well with the old adage not to trust a thin chef. A chef such as Bobbly Flay, who is renowned for his grilling abilities and skill cooking meat, could host Cooking U, a show which teaches the fundamentals of preparing homo sapiens. Ideally, the Culinary Institute of America would offer specialized courses in cannibalism, and hopefully add human cooking to its biblical tome The New Professional Chef. The dainty Martha Stewart might even be enlisted, as well as aficionados of exotic cuisine such as Anthony Bourdain.

Reality TV shows such as a Survivor spin-off would also be appropriate. In such a show, individuals without families would form a nomadic herd, engage in competitions, and the person voted out would be the one eaten that week. The Biggest Loser could also be toughened up and inculcate rugged individualism. It could be filmed in a least-developed country. The person who loses the most weight each week would win, but the person who loses the least would be fed to the hungry. It would be fascinating to observe emaciated residents of least-developed countries discovering morbidly obese Americans in Gods Must Be Crazy fashion.

Once again, these simple examples are only meant to illustrate feasibility; more sophisticated and effective marketing campaigns will most certainly be created by experts.

Once human processing plants are operational, they must conform to the highest standards of sanitation and quality control. Groups and agencies like People for the Ethical Treatment of

Animals (PETA) and the Food and Drug Administration (FDA) would have to be appraised of production methods. It may be necessary to create People for the Ethical Treatment of Humans (PETH), though it has been argued that such an organization is superfluous. Whatever the regulatory methodology, bootleg flesh could not be allowed. Plumper residents of developed nations, with their ability to produce more meat than two or three residents of least-developed countries, might be preyed upon during work or vacation in least-developed countries. Proper regulation of plants that process and export humans would be essential. This is especially important to ensure the integrity of human flesh marketed as organic. Unscrupulous manufacturers might try to pass off butchered non-organic residents of developed nations as organic. Consumers must have confidence in the integrity of human flesh that is marketed as organic.

The economic value generated by the sale of human products would bring a steady flow of wealth back into the countries of the survivors. This wealth could be used to build the aforementioned industries and infrastructure, modernizing least-developed countries.

The first few countries producing human flesh would enjoy a worldwide market domination that would for all practical purposes be a monopoly. This monopoly would not be indefinite, however. Eventually, numerous least-developed countries would begin exporting flesh and capitalistic laws of competition would come into play. Many impoverished countries would be competing against each other for limited market share. Though initial demand would probably swell due to novelty, corrections in the human flesh market would occur sooner or later. Who can say which tastes the world would prefer? The sinewy, more muscular meat of the Africans? Sweeter, pork-like Indians? Consumer preferences are often fickle, and capitalism scorned can be a cruel mistress indeed.

In a depressed market, families might have to sell two or three relatives to butcheries to earn revenue one might fetch in a healthier market. Over the long term, such short sightedness could be catastrophic, for women bear children at a fixed rate, and inventory might never be replenished sufficiently to restore previous levels. A supply-side economist I consulted felt that these concerns were overwrought, and that the barriers to production were sufficiently low that supply would remain robust even in the face of decreasing prices. Regardless, price would reflect scarcity, and increasing prices would probably create production fervors, making individual women little more than factories. The imbalance would be self-correcting, however, as each new baby would literally cheapen life.

To avoid such disasters, governments in least-developed countries would have to establish safeguards. This is reasonable. Developed nations set price floors and ceilings for their most fundamental agricultural commodities. Why should the burgeoning trade in the commodity that is homo sapiens be any different? Government has a sacred responsibility to prevent the cheapening of life and must take that responsibility seriously. Some would argue that human life is already the cheapest commodity on the planet and cannot be cheapened further, but we cannot afford to leave the matter to chance.

Like most prosperous nations in history, our cannibal country would be built by butchering humans. In such a nation, the ultimate store of value would not be precious metals or currency, but people. It is therefore logical that the monetary unit in such a nation would not be a dollar, euro, yen, or even a special quartering right, but a human.

When money was honest, it was defined by statute as a fixed weight of some commodity. For example, a dollar was legally defined as a fixed weight of gold or silver for most of American history, especially in the early days of the republic when government still served the people. Our cannibal nations would define their monetary unit as a fixed weight of human flesh, ideally a pound of flesh. This does create problems of uniformity, and to a lesser degree divisibility, both acknowledged attributes of optimal currency. All currencies fluctuate in value however, and instabilities introduced by non-uniformity, and to a lesser degree non-divisibility, will be minimal.

The advantages to making humans themselves the unit of exchange are multitudinous. As long as governments stayed on the "human standard," the stability of the money supply and prices, especially flesh prices, would be assured. Monetary policy by the government could not exist, for government could only create and destroy money by creating and destroying people. Though baby booms and plagues would create natural fluctuations in the money supply, hyperinflation and the economic woes that result from it would be eradicated as surely as malnutrition. Hyperdeflation, that scourge of ledgerized fiat money systems, and the cause of virtually every economic Depression in history, would also be virtually impossible under a human standard or human-exchange standard. My plan eradicates that kwashiorkor of the currency and marasmus of the money supply that has historically ravaged nations. The cannibal country would also stay out of debt, for it could always invoke a draft-like lottery system and ship out enough currency to settle delinquent accounts.

Subsisting-class citizens would also benefit from a human-standard monetary system. A family with children would always have credit. All families will be continuously capable of paying taxes and giving government its pound of flesh. Underclasses would be tough to create, for any family could create wealth by simply giving birth. Every member of a society would have capital in the form of their own person. A country built on the slaughter of humans that made humans its money would combine the great strengths of capitalism and socialism and be almost Utopian. At long last, the ideal espoused by philosophers and humanitarians throughout history would be realized. In such a nation, every human life would have intrinsic value!

The human butcher industry will be the cornerstone of what will eventually be a highly specialized modern economy. When this modernization has finally been achieved, the time for celebration will be at hand. Newly-developed nations will perhaps establish a holiday similar to America's Thanksgiving. Rather than thanking some third party who provided salvation, as Americans did with their kind treatment of the Indians, newly-developed nations will undoubtedly derive significant satisfaction from the fact that no external aid came. They will be glad that they did not become parasites impoverishing developed nations, and were not subjugated by that sinister dependence called charity, but rather succeeded on their own, through self-reliance. Like Americans, newly-developed nations will perhaps set up a commemorative feast to celebrate their good fortune. The ability to provide a feast where once there was only starvation will make such a holiday sacred. The fact that families will be feasting on a relative will make the holiday even more sacrosanct. One can picture sons and daughters that jockey for the auspicious honor of being the entrée on the day thanks is given.

This heart-warming holiday scene is an idyllic place to conclude. My proposal has been extrapolated far enough. Its benefits are numerous and plain to see. The bottom line is that this plan provides a method by which people presently starving will obtain sustenance.

It is unrealistic to assume a situation as severe as that in least-developed countries can be corrected quickly. We must be patient. It may take time, but in the end, the least-developed countries of today will enjoy the prosperity they deserve, and be the developed nations of tomorrow!

This proposal may seem extreme to some, but what other options, in light of the failure of prodigious efforts by developed nations, remain? Clearly, the $4 a week it takes to feed the resident of a least-developed country is an onerous sacrifice for the average resident of developed nations. Subtracting the aforementioned sum from the income of the average developed-nation resident would require reductions in standards of living that amount to cruel & unusual punishment. Residents of developed nations should not be expected to forsake a latte a week, much less the newest levitating 52G cellphone, nor endure a TV with mere 1080p rather than 4K, nor wear clothing that is not trendy, nor sup in some cramped kitchen without sprawling granite counters, nor suffer through a sporting event at some decadent seven-year-old stadium, nor drive a car without televisions and bling-bling rims, simply to save a few billion lives continents away. These necessities are the birthright of residents of developed nations, and it is unconscionable to ask them to sacrifice them at the altar of altruism. Had the lottery of birth location been swapped, and every developed-nation resident living in luxury was born in abject poverty in a least-developed country, they would not expect assistance, but rather would doubtless want the freedom to resolve the problem on their own without aid, obtaining the satisfaction derived thereof.

The tens of millions of malnourished who die each year do so with admirable dignity and fortitude, yet the reality that these deaths serve no purpose is inescapable. The essence of this proposal's humanity is that it gives meaning to otherwise futile lives. Given the choice between a senseless death, and one transformed and filled with purpose, what reasonable person can refuse someone the right to choose the latter? Individuals deserve a chance to leave the world nourishing loved ones, making meaningful contributions to fellow brothers and sisters of the tightly-knit family that is homo sapiens.

I offer this proposal humbly. Having no wife or children, no business ties in least-developed countries, and being a vegetarian, I have nothing to gain by its adoption. Except, of course, those benefits which must, if the plan is adopted, accrue to humanity as a whole.

A MODEST

PROPOSAL

Johnathan Swift

1792

A MODEST PROPOSAL

For Preventing the Children of Poor People in Ireland, from Being a Burden on their Parents or Country, and for Making them Beneficial to the Publick.

It is a melancholy object to those, who walk through this great town, or travel in the country, when they see the streets, the roads and cabbin-doors crowded with beggars of the female sex, followed by three, four, or six children, all in rags, and importuning every passenger for an alms. These mothers instead of being able to work for their honest livelihood, are forced to employ all their time in stroling to beg sustenance for their helpless infants who, as they grow up, either turn thieves for want of work, or leave their dear native country, to fight for the Pretender in Spain, or sell themselves to the Barbadoes.

I think it is agreed by all parties, that this prodigious number of children in the arms, or on the backs, or at the heels of their mothers, and frequently of their fathers, is in the present deplorable state of the kingdom, a very great additional grievance; and therefore whoever could find out a fair, cheap and easy method of making these children sound and useful members of the common-wealth, would deserve so well of the publick, as to have his statue set up for a preserver of the nation.

But my intention is very far from being confined to provide only for the children of professed beggars: it is of a much greater extent, and shall take in the whole number of infants at a certain age, who are born of parents in effect as little able to support them, as those who demand our charity in the streets.

As to my own part, having turned my thoughts for many years, upon this important subject, and maturely weighed the several schemes of our projectors, I have always found them grossly mistaken in their computation. It is true, a child just dropt from its dam, may be supported by her milk, for a solar year, with little other nourishment: at most not above the value of two shillings, which the mother may certainly get, or the value in scraps, by her lawful occupation of begging; and it is exactly at one year old that I propose to provide for them in such a manner, as, instead of being a charge upon their parents, or the parish, or wanting food and raiment for the rest of their lives, they shall, on the contrary, contribute to the feeding, and partly to the cloathing of many thousands.

There is likewise another great advantage in my scheme, that it will prevent those voluntary abortions, and that horrid practice of women murdering their bastard children, alas! too frequent among us, sacrificing the poor innocent babes, I doubt, more to avoid the expence than the shame, which would move tears and pity in the most savage and inhuman breast.

The number of souls in this kingdom being usually reckoned one million and a half, of these I calculate there may be about two hundred thousand couple whose wives are breeders; from which number I subtract thirty thousand couple, who are able to maintain their own children, (although I apprehend there cannot be so many, under the present distresses of the kingdom) but this being granted, there will remain an hundred and seventy thousand breeders. I again subtract fifty thousand, for those women who miscarry, or whose children die by accident or disease within the year. There only remain an hundred and twenty thousand children of poor parents annually born. The question therefore is, How this number shall be reared, and provided for? which, as I have already said, under the present situation of affairs, is utterly impossible by all the methods hitherto proposed. For we can neither employ them in handicraft or agriculture; they neither build houses, (I mean in the country) nor cultivate land: they can very seldom pick up a livelihood by stealing till they arrive at six years old; except where they are of towardly parts, although I confess they learn the rudiments much earlier; during which time they can however be properly looked upon only as probationers: As I have been informed by a principal gentleman in the county of Cavan, who protested to me, that he never knew above one or two instances under the age of six, even in a part of the kingdom so renowned for the quickest proficiency in that art.

I am assured by our merchants, that a boy or a girl before twelve years old, is no saleable commodity, and even when they come to this age, they will not yield above three pounds, or three pounds and half a crown at most, on the exchange; which cannot turn to account either to the parents or kingdom, the charge of nutriments and rags having been at least four times that value.

I shall now therefore humbly propose my own thoughts, which I hope will not be liable to the least objection.

I have been assured by a very knowing American of my acquaintance in London, that a young healthy child well nursed, is, at a year old, a most delicious nourishing and wholesome food, whether stewed, roasted, baked, or boiled; and I make no doubt that it will equally serve in a fricasie, or a ragout.

I do therefore humbly offer it to publick consideration, that of the hundred and twenty thousand children, already computed, twenty thousand may be reserved for breed, whereof only one fourth part to be males; which is more than we allow to sheep, black cattle, or swine, and my reason is, that these children are seldom the fruits of marriage, a circumstance not much regarded by our savages, therefore, one male will be sufficient to serve four females. That the remaining hundred thousand may, at a year old, be offered in sale to the persons of quality and fortune, through the kingdom, always advising the mother to let them suck plentifully in the last month, so as to render them plump, and fat for a good table. A child will make two dishes at an entertainment for friends, and when the family dines alone, the fore or hind quarter will make a reasonable dish, and seasoned with a little pepper or salt, will be very good boiled on the fourth day, especially in winter.

I have reckoned upon a medium, that a child just born will weigh 12 pounds, and in a solar year, if tolerably nursed, encreaseth to 28 pounds.

I grant this food will be somewhat dear, and therefore very proper for landlords, who, as they have already devoured most of the parents, seem to have the best title to the children.

Infant's flesh will be in season throughout the year, but more plentiful in March, and a little before and after; for we are told by a grave author, an eminent French physician, that fish being a prolifick dyet, there are more children born in Roman Catholick countries about nine months after Lent, the markets will be more glutted than usual, because the number of Popish infants, is at least three to one in this kingdom, and therefore it will have one other collateral advantage, by lessening the number of Papists among us.

I have already computed the charge of nursing a beggar's child (in which list I reckon all cottagers, labourers, and four-fifths of the farmers) to be about two shillings per annum, rags included; and I believe no gentleman would repine to give ten shillings for the carcass of a good fat child, which, as I have said, will make four dishes of excellent nutritive meat, when he hath only some par-ticular friend, or his own family to dine with him. Thus the squire will learn to be a good landlord, and grow popular among his tenants, the mother will have eight shillings neat profit, and be fit for work till she produces another child.

Those who are more thrifty (as I must confess the times require) may flea the carcass; the skin of which, artificially dressed, will make admirable gloves for ladies, and summer boots for fine gentlemen.

As to our City of Dublin, shambles may be appointed for this purpose, in the most convenient parts of it, and butchers we may be assured will not be wanting; although I rather recommend buying the children alive, and dressing them hot from the knife, as we do roasting pigs.

A very worthy person, a true lover of his country, and whose virtues I highly esteem, was lately pleased, in discoursing on this matter, to offer a refinement upon my scheme. He said, that many gentlemen of this kingdom, having of late destroyed their deer, he conceived that the want of venison might be well supply'd by the bodies of young lads and maidens, not exceeding fourteen years of age, nor under twelve; so great a number of both sexes in every country being now ready to starve for want of work and service: And these to be disposed of by their parents if alive, or otherwise by their nearest relations. But with due deference to so excellent a friend, and so deserving a patriot, I cannot be altogether in his sentiments; for as to the males, my American acquaintance assured me from frequent experience, that their flesh was generally tough and lean, like that of our school-boys, by continual exercise, and their taste disagreeable, and to fatten them would not answer the charge. Then as to the females, it would, I think, with humble submission, be a loss to the publick, because they soon would become breeders themselves: And besides, it is not improbable that some scrupulous people might be apt to censure such a practice, (although indeed very unjustly) as a little bordering upon cruelty, which, I confess, hath always been with me the strongest objection against any project, how well soever intended.

But in order to justify my friend, he confessed, that this expedient was put into his head by the famous Salmanaazor, a native of the island Formosa, who came from thence to London, above twenty years ago, and in conversation told my friend, that in his country, when any young person happened to be put to death, the executioner sold the carcass to persons of quality, as a prime dainty; and that, in his time, the body of a plump girl of fifteen, who was crucified for an attempt to poison the Emperor, was sold to his imperial majesty's prime minister of state, and other great mandarins of the court in joints from the gibbet, at four hundred crowns. Neither indeed can I deny, that if the same use were made of several plump young girls in this town, who without one single groat to their fortunes, cannot stir abroad without a chair, and appear at a play-house and assemblies in foreign fineries which they never will pay for; the kingdom would not be the worse.

Some persons of a desponding spirit are in great concern about that vast number of poor people, who are aged, diseased, or maimed; and I have been desired to employ my thoughts what course may be taken, to ease the nation of so grievous an incumbrance. But I am not in the least pain upon that matter, because it is very well known, that they are every day dying, and rotting, by cold and famine, and filth, and vermin, as fast as can be reasonably expected. And as to the young labourers, they are now in almost as hopeful a condition. They cannot get work, and consequently pine away from want of nourishment, to a degree, that if at any time they are accidentally hired to common labour, they have not strength to perform it, and thus the country and themselves are happily delivered from the evils to come.

I have too long digressed, and therefore shall return to my subject. I think the advantages by the proposal which I have made are obvious and many, as well as of the highest importance.

For first, as I have already observed, it would greatly lessen the number of Papists, with whom we are yearly over-run, being the principal breeders of the nation, as well as our most dangerous enemies, and who stay at home on purpose with a design to deliver the kingdom to the Pretender, hoping to take their advantage by the absence of so many good Protestants, who have chosen rather to leave their country, than stay at home and pay tithes against their conscience to an episcopal curate.

Secondly, The poorer tenants will have something valuable of their own, which by law may be made liable to a distress, and help to pay their landlord's rent, their corn and cattle being already seized, and money a thing unknown.

Thirdly, Whereas the maintainance of an hundred thousand children, from two years old, and upwards, cannot be computed at less than ten shillings a piece per annum, the nation's stock will be thereby encreased fifty thousand pounds per annum, besides the profit of a new dish, introduced to the tables of all gentlemen of fortune in the kingdom, who have any refinement in taste. And the money will circulate among our selves, the goods being entirely of our own growth and manufacture.

Fourthly, The constant breeders, besides the gain of eight shillings sterling per annum by the sale of their children, will be rid of the charge of maintaining them after the first year.

Fifthly, This food would likewise bring great custom to taverns, where the vintners will certainly be so prudent as to procure the best receipts for dressing it to perfection; and consequently have their houses frequented by all the fine gentlemen, who justly value themselves upon their knowledge in good eating; and a skilful cook, who understands how to oblige his guests, will contrive to make it as expensive as they please.

Sixthly, This would be a great inducement to marriage, which all wise nations have either encouraged by rewards, or enforced by laws and penalties. It would encrease the care and tenderness of mothers towards their children, when they were sure of a settlement for life to the poor babes, provided in some sort by the publick, to their annual profit instead of expence. We should soon see an honest emulation among the married women, which of them could bring the fattest child to the market. Men would become as fond of their wives, during the time of their pregnancy, as they are now of their mares in foal, their cows in calf, or sow when they are ready to farrow; nor offer to beat or kick them (as is too frequent a practice) for fear of a miscarriage.

Many other advantages might be enumerated. For instance, the addition of some thousand carcasses in our exportation of barrel'd beef: the propagation of swine's flesh, and improvement in the art of making good bacon, so much wanted among us by the great destruction of pigs, too frequent at our tables; which are no way comparable in taste or magnificence to a well grown, fat yearly child, which roasted whole will make a considerable figure at a Lord Mayor's feast, or any other publick entertainment. But this, and many others, I omit, being studious of brevity.

Supposing that one thousand families in this city, would be constant customers for infants flesh, besides others who might have it at merry meetings, particularly at weddings and christenings, I compute that Dublin would take off annually about twenty thousand carcasses; and the rest of the kingdom (where probably they will be sold somewhat cheaper) the remaining eighty thousand.

I can think of no one objection, that will possibly be raised against this proposal, unless it should be urged, that the number of people will be thereby much lessened in the kingdom. This I freely own, and 'twas indeed one principal design in offering it to the world. I desire the reader will observe, that I calculate my remedy for this one individual Kingdom of Ireland, and for no other that ever was, is, or, I think, ever can be upon Earth. Therefore let no man talk to me of other expedients: Of taxing our absentees at five shillings a pound: Of using neither cloaths, nor houshold furniture, except what is of our own growth and manufacture: Of utterly rejecting the materials and instruments that promote foreign luxury:

Of curing the expensiveness of pride, vanity, idleness, and gaming in our women: Of introducing a vein of parsimony, prudence and temperance: Of learning to love our country, wherein we differ even from Laplanders, and the inhabitants of Topinamboo: Of quitting our animosities and factions, nor acting any longer like the Jews, who were murdering one another at the very moment their city was taken: Of being a little cautious not to sell our country and consciences for nothing: Of teaching landlords to have at least one degree of mercy towards their tenants. Lastly, of putting a spirit of honesty, industry, and skill into our shop-keepers, who, if a resolution could now be taken to buy only our native goods, would immediately unite to cheat and exact upon us in the price, the measure, and the goodness, nor could ever yet be brought to make one fair proposal of just dealing, though often and earnestly invited to it.

Therefore I repeat, let no man talk to me of these and the like expedients, 'till he hath at least some glympse of hope, that there will ever be some hearty and sincere attempt to put them into practice.

But, as to my self, having been wearied out for many years with offering vain, idle, visionary thoughts, and at length utterly despairing of success, I fortunately fell upon this proposal, which, as it is wholly new, so it hath something solid and real, of no expence and little trouble, full in our own power, and whereby we can incur no danger in disobliging England. For this kind of commodity will not bear exportation, and flesh being of too tender a consistence, to admit a long continuance in salt, although perhaps I could name a country, which would be glad to eat up our whole nation without it.

After all, I am not so violently bent upon my own opinion, as to reject any offer, proposed by wise men, which shall be found equally innocent, cheap, easy, and effectual. But before something of that kind shall be advanced in contradiction to my scheme, and offering a better, I desire the author or authors will be pleased maturely to consider two points. First, As things now stand, how they will be able to find food and raiment for a hundred thousand useless mouths and backs. And secondly, There being a round million of creatures in humane figure throughout this kingdom, whose whole subsistence put into a common stock, would leave them in debt two million of pounds sterling, adding those who are beggars by profession, to the bulk of farmers, cottagers and labourers, with their wives and children, who are beggars in effect; I desire those politicians who dislike my overture, and may perhaps be so bold to attempt an answer, that they will first ask the parents of these mortals, whether they would not at this day think it a great happiness to have been sold for food at a year old, in the manner I prescribe, and thereby have avoided such a perpetual scene of misfortunes, as they have since gone through, by the oppression of landlords, the impossibility of paying rent without money or trade, the want of common sustenance, with neither house nor cloaths to cover them from the inclemencies of the weather, and the most inevitable prospect of intailing the like, or greater miseries, upon their breed for ever.

I profess, in the sincerity of my heart, that I have not the least personal interest in endeavouring to promote this necessary work, having no other motive than the publick good of my country, by advancing our trade, providing for infants, relieving the poor, and giving some pleasure to the rich. I have no children, by which I can propose to get a single penny; the youngest being nine years old, and my wife past child-bearing.

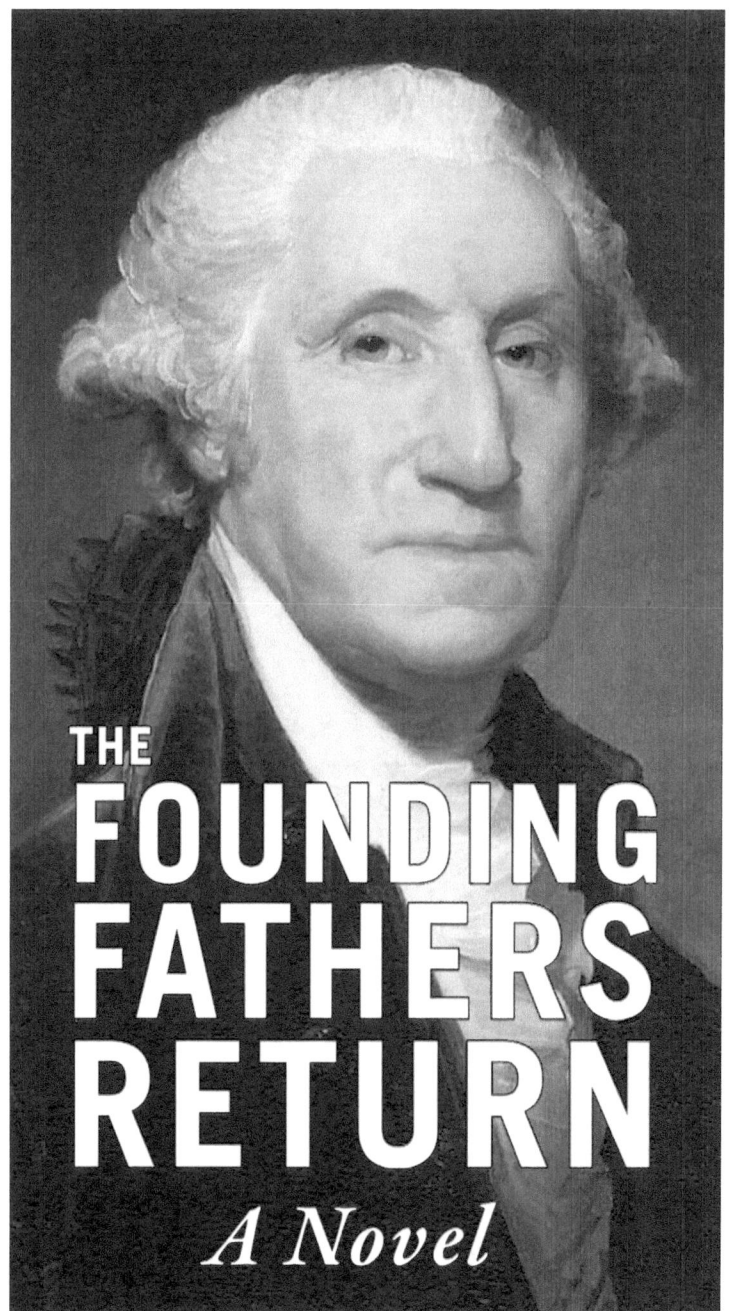

THE
FOUNDING
FATHERS
RETURN

A Novel

Please visit LawrenceRowe.com to learn more about
The Founding Fathers Return.